PAJAMA PANDA
PUBLISHING ™

SAVIORS OF CRIETAN
THE BEGINNING

By
L. E. M. Moss

CONTENTS

INTRODUCTION

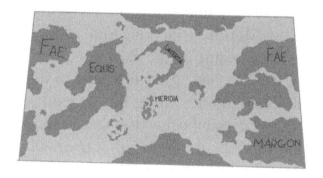

THIS is the story of a set of twins. This particular set of twins are Cerfinum, mystical beings who normally are gifted with an elemental power. They appear human but possess a pair of antlers and a tail, both resembling those of a deer . Sadly, these twins were born in a period of war.

Five years before the twins were born, Leio, the King of Margon, where all of the trolls and gremlins were from, decided his kingdom should have more territory, despite having almost the lowest population of all the five realms, second only to Lacerta. While at the annual peace meeting between the Five Realms of Crietan, he voiced this thought, but his proposal was shot down immediately by the other leaders. Infuriated, he struck an attack against the unicorn dynasty in Equis but died a shameful death in battle.

Another meeting was held amongst the leaders of Equis; the land of centaurs, unicorns, and other hoofed creatures, Meridia; the kingdom of the merpeople, Fae; the realm of the fairy folk, and Lacerta; land of the dragons, to decide what to do about the trolls of Margon. During this meeting, Prince Kree, son of Leio ambushed the delegation, killing all of the leaders, and declaring war on all Realms before returning home to be crowned king.

The trolls went through each realm one by one, taking over whichever villages they could find. One of those villages happened to be Arietes, the village in Equis on the outskirts of which two of our heroes were born. And so, our story begins.

CHAPTER 1

ATTACKED

"FAUN! Check out this new trick!" exclaimed Flicker. He pulled his goggles down over his eyes, pulled off the blacksmith's gloves which he always wore to prevent himself from burning others, and reached his hand into the fireplace. He pulled a ball of fire out, which he then began to juggle between his hands.

"You'll set the house on fire," said Faun, who was too focused on the small stone golem she was attempting to make to be enthused.

"You're just jealous because my power is cooler than yours."

"Flicker!" exclaimed their mother.

Faun stood calmly, walked over to the stone fireplace, and banged her fist against it, rocking the house and sending a chip of stone flying right into the middle of Flicker's forehead.

"Hey!" he shouted.

"Oops!" she said innocently. "I must have been distracted by the sheer awesomeness of your power!" She began to laugh uncontrollably.

"Faun!" shouted their mother.

"Sorry," she giggled.

"Not cool Faun," he groaned, rubbing his bruised forehead. He looked over at the mantle of the fireplace and gasped. "You knocked over dad's picture!" He set the picture upright and sighed.

Their father had left to fight in the war a few weeks after the twins' eighth birthday and had promised them that he would soon return. They counted every day after he left, but soon the days turned into weeks, and the weeks into months, and soon they had lost count, but they never lost hope that their father would return.

"Mom?" Faun asked, turning to her mother.

"Yes, my love?" came her Mother's exhausted response.

"When's dad coming home?"

A completely different mood had set over the room, and the once cheerful atmosphere turned into a sombre and silent one. Her mother sighed, her sorrow dimming the room.

"I... I don't know, love."

"But I-"

"BANG! BANG! BANG!" came a loud knock at the door.

A look of distress fell over their mother's face. "Go into your room children," she said, attempting to mask her worry. She walked over to their money box and picked it up. "And lock the door."

They picked up their belongings, hurried into their room and locked the door behind them just as they were told.

Faun pressed her ear to the door, hoping to hear a bit of conversation, but couldn't make out anything her mother was saying.

"It's no use," said Flicker, who was now digging through things underneath his bed. He was flinging things left and right in his search for something or other to entertain him. "You can't hear a thing from behind this door."

Faun turned away from the door and sat with her back pressed against it. She sighed and said, "I just wish I knew what was going on. We aren't babies anymore, Flick. We're twelve years old! I think that's old enough to be included in these kinds of things."

"But you know what's going on," he said. "Those stupid trolls come, collect their stupid tax, then leave, carrying their stupid stupidity with them. There's nothing else to it."

Faun sighed and decided to watch her brother as he searched for... whatever it was that he was searching for. She couldn't tell. After all, he had already pulled out stones, socks with no matching pairs, a half-eaten... something, and some old toys. He looked at them for a while, then flung them off to the side and continued to dig.

"How do you have so much junk underneath your bed?" she asked. "We have trunks to put our things in to avoid this mess."

"Well," Flicker started, "my trunk is where I keep my underwear."

"Wait. If your trunk is full of underwear then what's in your drawer?"

"My drawer?" he asked. "That's where I used to keep my pet turtle-slugs." At this point, he was just flinging things. He decided he'd look through those things later.

"You're disgusting," she gagged.

"Likewise," quipped Flicker.

Something went flying in Faun's direction from under the bed and landed right beside her. She picked it up and studied it. It was made of some sort of soft fabric, and red and green in colour, and after a closer look, she realised that it was actually two objects intertwined with each other instead of just one. Her eyes widened in surprise as she pulled the two items apart. "Flick! These are the hats that dad gave us before he left!"

Flicker got up in an instant, forgetting that he was underneath the bed, and hit his head with a loud "THUD!" Faun snickered, much to his annoyance as he crawled over to her rubbing his head and took the red hat from her hands.

He looked at the hat nostalgically before sliding it over his small, newly forming antlers, leaving only a small tuft of his messy chestnut brown hair peeking out from beneath it, then sat and did the same for her.

Faun poked at the goggles he wore. "How can you see through those thick goggles?" she asked.

He got up and brought her a pair of goggles from his drawer. "See for yourself," he said, pulling them over her head.

They went over to the mirror to look at themselves. They looked exactly alike. They had the same coloured hair, the same freckled cheeks, and the same dimple that only appeared on the left side of each twin's face. If Faun were to hide her pigtails underneath her hat, you probably wouldn't be able to tell the two apart.

"Hey, Flick? It's been a while. They normally just take the money and leave. And it's getting kinda hot in here. Do you think we should--"?

"Go check?" he interrupted, "I was just having the same thought."

She stepped aside, and he opened the door to see raging flames filling up the living room. They looked on in horror and disbelief as the beautiful home they once knew was being burnt to a crisp.

"Hold on to me," Flicker demanded.

Faun did as she was told. He cleared a path for them to walk through the fire. The burnt wooden floor cried out from beneath them with every step they took, and the blistering heat of the blaze was unbearable. They ran outside, only to find

Margonian soldiers shackling their mother and preparing to carry her off as a prisoner.

"Mom..." Faun quavered, short of breath. She pulled the goggles up onto her forehead and hid behind Flicker.

"Let go of her!" screamed Flicker. The rage in him burned like the flames that consumed their home.

The youngest of the soldiers turned to the others. He was actually quite handsome and well-groomed for a troll and had on different armour than the others. "Go on without me," he said maniacally as an evil smirk grew on his face. "I'll catch up after I'm done with these two."

Their mother screamed and cried as the unsightly trolls carried her off into the distance, and soon the twins could hear her no longer.

"Now children," the soldier gently intoned, stepping closer to them, "Don't be afraid. I won't hurt your mother. She just couldn't pay her taxes, so we had to take her."

Flicker glared at him and dropped his gloves into the grass. "What do you mean, 'couldn't pay her taxes?' I know we had more than enough bits to pay your stupid tax!"

"I'd watch your tone if I were you, boy," the soldier snapped. "Anyways, there was a surprise double tax today! Isn't that fun?"

Tears began to well in Faun's eyes.

"Don't cry little doe! Keep your head high!" smiled the soldier sarcastically, as he raised her chin.

"Don't touch her!" Flicker shouted, slapping his hand away.

The soldier grabbed him by the shirt collar and raised him off of the ground. "Don't test me, little boy."

Flicker swung his hand and instantly, fire shot from the roof down to the soldier who screamed, grabbing his neck where he had been burned immediately letting him go.

Flicker swiftly picked up his gloves and put them on as he ran over to Faun and grabbed her wrist. "Let's go!" he yelled.

They ran off into the forest and didn't stop until they were sure they were far enough from their house that the trolls wouldn't find them, and soon fell asleep in the hollow stump of a tree, wrapped in each other's arms.

CHAPTER 2

SEPARATED

"FLICKER... Flicker!" Faun said, shaking her brother.

"Hm?" he said groggily.

"We need to go check out the house."

He looked at her and nodded silently. He stood, and together, they walked through the forest to the burnt remains of their home.

They stepped onto the ash covered floor. Everything they had ever known had been destroyed, and neither of them knew how to process it.

Faun walked into their bedroom. She reached under what was left of her bed and pulled out her trunk from underneath. Inside of it, her possessions had been kept safe from the fire. She opened the trunk and began to search through her things. She stopped all of a sudden and pulled out a locket. Inside of one half was a picture of her and Flicker, and the other was a picture of their parents. She pulled it over her head and opened it, staring at the picture of her father. She then reached inside and pulled out a satchel that also belonged to their father.

Flicker went over to where the money box was. He turned it over, only to see that it was empty except for two copper bits. He walked over to the fireplace and found what was once a picture of their father. He placed it where it used to be and removed his glove. He then closed his eyes, placing his hand on the stone. After a while, he opened his eyes, taking in one last look, put his glove back on and walked outside. He was soon joined by Faun, who had tucked the locket into her shirt, so he couldn't see it.

"I should've stopped it," said Flicker, seemingly lost in thought while staring at the wall.

"What?" asked Faun.

"The fire," he said, turning to her. "I should've stopped it."

"Don't be ridiculous," said Faun. "You know your powers aren't strong enough yet to have done that."

He turned back towards the roofless house. He hardly even blinked.

"It's not your fault, you know. You tried to save her."

He looked at Faun for a moment, then turned and began to walk towards the forest.

"Where are you going?" she asked.

"To finish what I started," he replied then stopped. "I'm going to save Mom."

Faun ran behind him and placed her hand on his shoulder. "Not without me," she said.

They started off into the forest, following the trail of trampled grass left there by the soldiers from the night before. They walked for miles, almost completely in silence, each thinking about nothing other than their mother.

"Hey!" came a shout from behind them. They turned to face the same soldier from last night. They knew it was him from the burn that was on the right side of his face and neck that was given to him by Flicker.

"Well if it isn't my two favourite nuisances," he smirked. He turned and shouted something in Margonian, and three other trolls showed up behind him.

"Make some fire!" Faun whispered.

"I can't!" Flicker shot back. "I don't know how!"

"What do you plan to do without your precious fire, boy? Are you going to boar me with those dangerously pointy antlers of yours?" he chuckled. He then turned to his soldiers and said, "Get them."

Immediately, the others ran towards them. The twins broke off running, not knowing where they were headed. Before they knew it, they were running across a bed of stone at the bottom of a cliff. They were cornered. One of the men came forward and began to reach out his hand to grab them.

Faun jumped in front of her brother, shut her eyes, and attempted to block him. She heard the three men grunt heavily followed by a thud. She opened her eyes to see them on the floor, and large stone pillars raised out of the ground in front of them.

"I did that?" she asked in disbelief.

"Awesome," exclaimed Flicker.

"Awesome indeed," said the burned soldier, who was now mere feet before them.

"Flicker run!" she screamed as she turned to run.

"Wait," said the soldier with a sinister smile. "Don't you want to know where your mother is?"

Both twins stopped in their tracks.

"Allow me to introduce myself," he said. "My name is Prince Kaye of Margon, eldest son of Kree."

"Yeah, that's nice," said Flicker monotonously. "Now where's my Mom?"

"Someone's a little cranky," Kaye teased, "Did baby not get his nap?" He laughed, seeming to enjoy their anguish. "Your mother," he started, "is at a prison camp for people like her who don't understand the importance of paying taxes to my father. It makes no sense going after her. Even if you find the place, you'll never find her. Besides, you'll see her whenever we decide to let her out.

That is, if we ever let her out. It's all in the details."
The prince laughed maniacally.

The twins glared at him. Neither could believe that he actually found joy in this.

"Ooh! Here's a thought! I could take you there now!" He pulled out a pair of chains and began walking towards them.

They bolted past him and began running back through the forest, but Kaye was right behind them. Faun stepped on a massive rock in the ground, which then shot up and hit the prince in the stomach. He fell to the floor holding his stomach and groaning and the twins ran off deeper into the forest.

CHAPTER 3

ALLIANCE

THEY both considered their last confrontation a success, although for different reasons. Faun felt it to be a success because she was actually able to use her powers in a way which she had never been able to before. She now wanted to test what else she could do. Flicker thought it to be a success because they now knew where their mother was. They just had to figure out how to get there.

As Flicker and Faun continued walking, they grew hungry. Luckily for them, they could hear a crowd of people in the distance. That meant there was a village nearby. They began running towards the sound, until they got to the village. It was a big one, with many vendors selling various items. The twins walked in and were taken aback by all of the buildings and stalls. They questioned how they would get food.

Flicker sighed. "Faun, I know you won't like this but-"

"I know. I know," she sighed. "We're gonna have to steal it."

They walked back and forth, discussing the plan. They had to make sure that the plan would work, strategically targeting the produce stall they would steal from.

Faun ran over to the vendor in tears. "I'm sorry to bother you, sir, but..." she began to cry a bit more heavily. "Have you... have you seen... my mother?"

While she did this, Flicker crept up behind the stall and grabbed a few things, dropping them into the satchel. He was so impressed by Faun's acting that he wasn't properly watching what he was doing. He reached up to grab one last star-pear, but the stack fell. Flicker tried to make a bolt for it. Faun, seeing this, did the same, but when she got to a safe distance away, she turned to see that her brother was struggling to get away from the vendor's grip.

"Let go of me!" he yelled trying to pull away from the vendor. He kicked and screamed and pulled, but nothing worked.

She stomped her foot, lifting a rock into the air, then gestured a punch in an attempt to send it flying their way, but it was pointless. The rock simply dropped. She watched in despair as they took him away.

Faun stood, clueless as to what she should do. She couldn't go home. There wasn't anything there to go home to. And she knew she couldn't go find their mother without Flicker. She sat with her back against the wall and hugged her knees.

"Hey, kid!" she heard a voice say.

Faun looked up to see an older girl in front of her. She studied the girl curiously, as she had neither antlers nor hooves. She had braids on the left side of her head, but her dark brown hair was loose and flowing everywhere else. She wasn't from Equis and didn't look like she was from Meridia, which was the closest realm to them at the moment.

Two boys walked out of the shadows followed by another girl who looked to be about Faun's age.

One of the boys was a centaur. He was built, and had long, brown locks that reached down to his back. The other was a merboy with short curly Auburn hair and violet eyes. As for the younger girl, she had long greyish violet hair that stopped at her shoulders.

"I'm Xi," said the first girl. "That's Brutus, Lucky and Xoe," she said, motioning to the centaur, the merboy, and then the girl. She extended her hand towards Faun.

"Oh... I'm Faun," she said timidly, gripping her hand and pulling herself up.

"We wanna help you find your brother," she said.

"How?"

"Well," Xi started, pulling a wand out of her boot, "it's simple. Follow me. I'll explain on the way."

"Where are we going?" asked Faun.

"Our hideout."

They walked for about half a mile through the forest until they reached a gargantuan Kodee- Nut Tree.

"Here we are," said Xi.

Faun looked up to see where the treetop was, but she could see nothing that looked like a hideout.

"Where is it?"

Xi laughed and once again pulled out her wand. "Up."

She waved the wand. Everything went black, and Faun felt herself seem to flatten and lose dimension. Suddenly, she felt herself shoot up and in an instant, she was standing inside a huge treehouse. She fell to the floor and attempted to catch her breath.

Xi looked at her, trying to keep herself from laughing. "Sorry, kid. I should've given you more warning." She chuckled, much to Faun's annoyance. "Let me help you up."

They sat on the floor and began to discuss how they would get Flicker back. After a while, they had finally decided on a plan.

"So, we're all clear on the plan?" asked Xi, standing.

"Yup," said Brutus.

"Yes," said Lucky.

Xoe and Faun nodded.

"Good. Now rest up. We leave at midnight."

"Midnight?" Faun interjected. "We can't wait 'til midnight! We have to go now!"

"No," Xi opposed. "If we go now, we won't have the element of surprise, but if we wait,"

"We will have the darkness to hide us from the enemy. We will have a better chance of achieving our goal if we wait," said Lucky, who was standing in the doorway about to walk off.

"And besides," said Brutus, standing up, "she's the leader. She says something, it goes. Boss knows what she's doing."

The boys bade her goodnight and walked over to the branch where they slept.

Faun stood and walked over to the window and stared at the sun setting behind the sea of trees around them. Xi walked over and joined her.

"Nice treehouse," Faun said, attempting to divert her from her intended conversation topic.

"Thanks," Xi replied.

"Hey, Xi? I have a question."

"Shoot."

"Well," she started, "what are you? I, I mean, not to be rude, but, well, you're not a troll, you're not a Meridian, a Lacertan, a Faerian, or an Equistrian. Are you like, some kind of tall elf with less pointy ears?"

Xi chuckled. "I'm a witch... from Margon... None of the witches wanted any part of the war, so they all left. They split up, going all across the globe. My mother decided to come here. When I was four years old, the king found our settlement and he took everybody to prison for 'treason', but somehow they never found me. A centaur, Brutus' dad, rescued me and Xoe, and took us in as his own. Xoe was a baby, so he named her as though we were sisters."

"Where is he now?" asked Faun.

Xi looked off to the side, a wave of sadness crashing over her. "He died... fighting in the war..."

"Oh... I'm sorry..." said Faun, who was wholeheartedly regretting asking that question.

"No, no. It's fine." She replied.

They stared at the night sky in silence. They looked at the two moons in the sky; Xenox, the glass moon (or so it was called for its translucency), and Ta'ela, the moon with many stars, which was named for the ring of stars which surrounded it. Faun watched a panda owl perch in a nearby tree. He looked at her and hooted a hello before flying off. It was so quiet that Faun could hear her own heartbeat.

Xi suddenly broke the silence. "He's going to be fine you know," she said softly. "Your brother I mean. He looks like a kid who can handle himself."

"Yeah," said Faun, "He is." She paused and sighed. "But I'm not."

"What?"

"I'm not strong or brave like him. And he's so much more talented than me. And his powers are amazing! I don't even know how mine work..."

"So, figure them out."

She turned and sat, sliding her back down the wall and sighed. "You say that like it's easy."

Xi looked down at her. "Do you think I got this good at magic overnight? Two years ago, if I had tried to teleport all those people at once, I'd have ripped us in half."

Faun looked away from her.

"All it takes is practice, kid. You'll get the hang of your powers. You just gotta give them time."

Faun looked up at her and smiled.

"Now get some rest. We strike at midnight."

Faun walked across the tree branch between the two rooms, over to where the boys were, and fell asleep.

CHAPTER 4

ESCAPE

"GET UP", said Xi, walking into the room. "It's time."

They all got up and prepared themselves to leave. The moon was at its peak, and the midnight air filled them with energy.

When they arrived at the edge of the forest, Xi turned to the others.

"Alright kid, you're up," she said. "Lucky, Xoe, Get in position."

Xoe and Lucky ran into the light, and Faun stomped her foot and gestured her hand forward, sending a small rock into the air and bouncing off of a metal sign, hitting the guard who sat sleeping outside of the village's small jail where Flicker was being held.

"Hey!" he shouted. He saw Lucky and Xoe and began to chase them as they ran away laughing.

Faun, Brutus and Xi ran to the jail door.

"Brutus?" said Xi.

"Standing guard," he replied.

Xi peeked inside, then crept in with Faun close on her tail. They began to search the cells for Flicker.

"Xi!" Faun whisper-shouted, "I found him!"

Xi ran over to her and nodded. "Good work. Now wake him up."

"Flick! Flicker!" she whispered. Upon realising that wouldn't work, she banged her fist against the stone wall, sending a stone flying into Flicker's forehead.

"Ah!" he said, opening his eyes.

"Quiet, you big dummy!" whispered Faun, "You'll get us caught!"

"Faun!" he whispered. "I didn't think you'd come for me!"

"Me? Leave you behind? That's funny."

"But you know what wouldn't be funny?" interrupted Xi. "Getting caught by that fatso. Let's save the 'sibling bonding time' 'til we're in the clear."

The twins nodded and they all crept outside.

"This is him?" said Brutus.

They nodded

"Then let's go."

They turned to leave, but suddenly there was an explosion of purple smoke in the distance, and soon enough, they could see Xoe and Lucky bolting towards them. Xoe ran right into Xi's arms and stared back at the source of the explosion.

Xi looked her in the eye. "What did you do?"

"Well," Xoe started, "he was gaining on us, and... I got scared, so... I tried to freeze him, but... but I said pullulate instead of glacio, and-"

"He multiplied..."

Suddenly, a herd of about ten of the same guard came rushing around the corner and charging straight for them.

They bolted. Lucky raised his hands and the water rose out of the fountain in the middle of the village. He swung his hands down swiftly, sending the water crashing down onto the men. Brutus pulled Xoe onto his back, and Lucky was standing on a wave that was pushing him forward much faster than he could run.

Flicker spun around. "Um, guys?"

"What is it?" asked Xi.

"Weren't there ten of those guys?"

They all turned to see only five of them in pursuit.

"So where are the other five?"

They looked around. The guards had circled them.

Xi swung her wand and shouted, "Couno!" but the wand only sparked and sputtered. "No!" she exclaimed. "My wand's out of juice!"

Xoe did the same, but the result was no different.

The guards rushed in and grabbed the children, who were struggling and trying to fight them off.

"Faun!" shouted Lucky, who was unable to use his power as there was no water around. "You are the only one of us still able to use your powers!"

"But-" she tried to interject.

"But nothing, kid!" interrupted Xi, elbowing one of the guards in the stomach. "We saved your brother! Now we need you to save us!"

Faun stomped her foot, but her nerves got the better of her, and nothing happened.

"Any time now!" yelled Brutus, who was kicking around wildly trying to get them off of him.

"I'm trying!" Faun replied.

"C'mon, Faun!" shouted Flicker. He ripped his glove off and placed his hand on one guard's arm, burning him. "We need you!"

Faun screamed, stomping her foot one last time. Suddenly, the ground began to shake. The ground beneath the guards' feet raised them high into the air.

"Run!" she shouted.

The others did as they were told, and as they reached the forest, they heard a crash. They all stopped and looked back, except for Faun.

"Let's go!" she yelled as she ran into the forest, and the others without a word followed her back.

The walk back to the hideout was silent, aside from the crunching leaves beneath their feet, the frequent squeaks of many little fox mice and the occasional panda owl, cooing softly.

By the time they got back to the tree, Xi and Xoe had just enough magic to get them all up. None of them said a word, and they all went to sleep.

The next morning, Faun woke up to see Flicker packing food into the satchel, and the others conversing in the corner. Xi looked over at Faun.

"Morning, sleeping beauty." she said, taking a few blank maps from a barrel and placing them into a bag. "Your brother told me where you guys are going. I'm coming with."

"But what about the others?"

"They'll be alright, and besides. It's not like I'm leaving forever." She paused and looked back at them. "We should probably leave soon if we wanna make good time."

They gathered their supplies and bade the others goodbye. Without looking back, the three ventured out into the forest, headed straight for Margon.

CHAPTER 5

STRANDED

"HEY! Watch it!" yelled Flicker, dodging a rock that flew past his head.

"I'm sorry!" said Faun.

They were on the western shore of Equis, and Faun was practicing use of her powers while Xi and Flicker tried to build the boat that they would use to get to Margon.

"Focus," said Xi. "Try closing your eyes. Picture yourself doing it."

As Faun closed her eyes, Xi pulled out her wand.

"Go!" she said.

Faun stomped her foot, and Xi whispered, "subvolo," causing a piece of earth to slowly float into the air.

"I did it!" Faun screamed with excitement.

"Yeah, kid. You did." Xi lied.

They heard a pile of wood drop to the floor.

"If you two are finished," said Flicker

"You've got the wood?" asked Xi.

"Yeah. Thanks for the help."

"It was no trouble at all," she replied, walking towards him. She circled around the pile of logs.

"They're big enough right?"

"Just barely. Stand back. It's gonna be big."

Flicker walked closer to her and whispered, "You can't lie to her forever."

"What?"

"Faun. I know you lifted that rock. Not her."

"Yeah, and? It was just a little confidence boost. Now step aside before you get hit with a flying log."

They all walked a safe distance away from the pile.

Xi raised her wand. "Pullulate! Aedificare navem!" she shouted.

The twins watched on in awe as the wood multiplied itself and turned into a boat before their very eyes.

"And there goes what was left of my magic," she said, spinning around. "I have to let my wand recollect itself for a few hours."

"Welp," said Flicker, "No time to waste. Let's go."

Everyone boarded the ship, and they set out. Night had fallen by this time, and they were all tired. Flicker was beneath deck sleeping, Faun was in the crow's nest reading the map and navigating, and Xi was steering the ship. They were giggling and telling stories as they worked, and Faun, for the first time since that night, felt like a normal girl.

"Really?" giggled Xi.

"Yeah!" Faun snorted while laughing. "And our mom was all like 'Finley! Get back here!'"

"Finley?"

"Yeah. Flicker's just a nickname, because when he first got his powers, all he could do was make sparks and tiny fires. So, our dad called him Flicker. The name just kinda stuck, I guess."

"Cute. What if I called him by his real name?"

"He'd go absolutely crazy. He doesn't like— AH!" The boat shook violently, sending Faun flying off. Just before she hit the deck, she stopped, suspended only an inch or two above, then dropped softly to the floor.

She got up and looked over at Xi, whose wand was still pointed at her.

"Thanks," said Faun as she got up.

"No problem."

They looked over at the side of the boat, which now had a gaping hole in its side, and was taking on lots of water. Then they looked into the distance and saw a Margonian ship that was preparing to launch another cannonball.

Flicker ran above deck screaming, "We've been hit! Xi! Can you fix it?"

She raised her wand, and shouted, "instaurabo!" but the wand did nothing more than spark. "Shoot!" she yelled. "I only had enough to save Faun!"

"What do we do now?" asked Faun.

The trio looked up to see two brightly flaming balls heading their way.

"We jump!" screamed Xi.

They jumped off of the boat just in time not to be caught in the explosion, but Faun, the last to jump off, was rendered unconscious by the impact.

Faun woke up covered in sand and soaking wet. She started coughing until water came out of her mouth.

"Faun!" shouted Flicker, who was stooped over a small pile of logs attempting to create a fire. "Thank goodness!"

"Welcome back, kid," said Xi.

She sat up, and looked around squinting, completely out of it. Her ears were ringing and filled with water, and she could barely see. "My head hurts..." she groaned.

"You hit it on a rock," replied Xi. "You've been out cold for hours."

"Where are we?"

"Some random island between Equis and Margon I guess," said Flicker. "And the sun's gonna set soon, too. This is great. Just—" he froze and stared at the bushes behind the beach as they shook softly. "Did you guys hear that?"

Xi smirked and chuckled softly. "Don't be paranoid, Sparky. It's probably just the wind."

The rustling got louder, and the bushes began to shake more than before.

Flicker looked at the girls. "Just the wi--"

"Hello, children," came a soft, creaky voice from the bushes.

The three screamed and held each other, but upon looking up, Xi pushed the other two off of her. When Faun opened her eyes, she saw a beautiful older lady of about eighty years old. She was a Cerfinum with brown skin, bright blue eyes and long white hair pulled back into a wild curly ponytail hung over her shoulder.

She walked over to Faun and looked at her with nostalgic eyes.

"Um, ma'am?" asked Faun. "Are you alright?"

"Oh, yes! Sorry, it's just—oh, never mind. It's getting late. You kids shouldn't be out here all by yourselves. My name is Azure. I have a little cottage with two extra rooms. Why don't you all come with me?"

They all felt strongly against going into a stranger's home, but they were wet, cold, and hungry, and had no better ideas so they followed her into the forest.

They soon came upon a large stone house. It was a bit bigger than Faun and Flicker's house.

"I thought you said a little cottage!" exclaimed Flicker.

Azure chuckled, causing the corners of her eyes to wrinkle even more. "Follow me, children."

They entered a grand hall, with doors scattered all about. The walls were covered in pictures.

"This place gives me the creeps," whispered Xi.

"I think it's amazing," said Faun, who was staring in awe at the many pictures that lined the walls as her eyesight had finally cleared up. She stopped abruptly, causing Xi to walk into her, and both girls fell to the floor.

"Watch it, kid," said Xi, standing up.

Azure and Flicker turned to face them.

"Sorry, but"—Faun pointed to one of the pictures on the wall "you knew our Grandmother, Lavender! Didn't you?" she paused. "You... look just like her. It's almost as though she were your..." She turned and looked at Azure in disbelief.

"My twin sister," she confirmed, a smile on her face. "We were identical, except her eyes were violet. If she was your grandmother... that means that your names are Faun and Finley!"

Xi exploded with laughter, but Faun tried her best to conceal her own giggles, causing them to sound like a more abrupt gust of air through her nose. Flicker, covered his face to hide his embarrassment. "Uh... Flicker," he mumbled.

"What was that, dear?" asked a slightly confused Azure.

"My name," he said with a bit more volume. "Most people just call me Flicker."

"Oh," she replied. "My apologies, *Flicker*. And what would your friend's name be?"

"Xi," replied Xi, who was still snickering under her breath.

"A pleasure to meet you Xi," Azure continued. "Now, I'm sure you're all starved. Allow me to show you to the kitchen."

After eating and telling their grand aunt of their travels, the children were shown to their rooms, and they fell soundly asleep.

CHAPTER 6

SOARING

"TAKE THIS," Azure said, handing them a large basket of food. "It's for your journey."

"Thank you," said Faun. "But I don't know how we'll even get there. Our ship is destroyed."

"Not to worry. Follow me."

They walked with her around to the back of the cottage. They stopped, only after arriving at an enormous structure that looked somewhat like a large stable. Azure walked up to the door and opened it.

As they all took a step into the darkness of the musty, weathered stable, Flicker scrunched his nose at the indiscreet aroma of a barn animal. "Why are we here, again?" he asked.

Suddenly, they all heard a loud snort, stopping them all in their tracks.

"Nero? Come out here," said Azure, much to the others' confusion.

Suddenly, a beautiful white and brown creature emerged from the darkness. It was bigger than all of them put together, and had the head and wings of an owl, but a body similar to that of a lion.

"This is my owl griffin, Nero," she said. "He will be able to take you there and bring you back."

They thanked her, and they all walked to the beach. After saying their goodbyes, Azure issued them one last warning before they left.

"Please be careful," she admonished. "The Margonian soldiers you will meet will not hold back just because you are children. Don't have a second thought about doing what you must to get away from them." She then looked at them with a soft look in her eyes and smiled. "Good luck children."

With that, they were off. They saddled up Nero and flew away from the island. They sat in the saddle, the brisk sea air blowing against their face. Xi was reading the map and directing Flicker, who was flying Nero.

Faun looked over the edge of the saddle at the waves rolling past them, or so it seemed. They were flying so fast that she truly couldn't tell. She wondered if she would be able to see a mermaid from so high up. Not like they would ever expose themselves like that though. The merfolk went completely into hiding at the start of the war. Most of them lived on land among the creatures of the other realms.

Faun was also nervous that she wouldn't be of much help once they finally got to the prison. She still wasn't in complete control of her powers. Even if she did manage to improve them while there, she still wouldn't be able to compare herself to Flicker, who, even when he was unable to use his powers, was so brave that to his sister, he seemed fearless, or to Xi, who was able to use her magic almost flawlessly. She was practically useless compared to them. She picked a pebble from her boot as she thought.

Faun, while playing with the pebble between her fingers was almost tempted to ask, *"Are we there yet?"* for the millionth time. She exhaled a heavy sigh and peered over the edge of the saddle once again, but this time noticing that she could just barely make out the outline of the gloomy Margonian shore in the distance.

"Land!" she shouted, standing up. "We're almost there, Mom," she whispered to herself.

Xi put down the map and opened her bag. She took out a small gem, looked inside of the bag and began to mumble something into it.

Faun turned around and looked at her. "Did you say something?" she asked, crawling towards her.

Xi shut the bag quickly. "Oh! Um... I just said that I'm glad that we'll be on solid ground again soon. I'm starting to get a little air sick. That's all."

"Oh-- is your bag glowing?"

Xi kicked the bag behind her. "I think you should've gotten a bit more sleep last night," she chuckled.

"Going in for a landing!" Flicker shouted.

"Flick! Look out!" shouted Faun and a large flaming boulder came hurtling their way.

Xi squeezed the gem in the palm of her hand.

Flicker stuck out his hands immediately extinguishing the fire, and Faun without a second thought leaped in front of Flicker and put her hands out, inadvertently throwing the pebble from her boot out towards it.

The pebble, upon impact, burst the rock into hundreds of pieces, but before they had time to celebrate, about twenty more flaming boulders came flying their way.

"There's no way you guys can take on all of those!" exclaimed Xi. She grabbed the reins and steered them to the top of a mountain, all while skilfully dodging the flaming projectiles.

As soon as they landed, Faun jumped off of Nero's back and excitedly shouted, "Did you guys see that? I broke the rock without touching it!"

"I wonder how they even found us," Flicker pondered. "Xi, do you have any idea?"

"Not a clue," she replied.

"Well, there goes our element of surprise," Flicker sighed. He stomped his foot and groaned, sending small flames out from under his foot.

Faun sighed. "It's okay. We'll still get her back. I'm sure of it."

Flicker created a small fire with wood, and they all ate from the basket Azure gave them and fell asleep there.

Later that night, Faun woke up. She heard something and turned over to see that Flicker was not in his sleeping bag. She found him with Nero, seemingly ready to take off.

"What are you doing?" she asked, startling him.

"N-Nothing," he stammered. "Go back to bed."

"Were you trying to leave without us?"

"No! Why would you think that?"

"Because you're on the back of an owl griffin with the map in the middle of the night. It doesn't take a genius."

"Fine... so what if I was leaving without you guys? I can do it on my own!"

"Stop thinking you can do everything on your own coz you can't! Why won't you let me help you?"

"Because I'm scared! I'm scared that I'm not strong enough..."

"And this is supposed to make you stronger?"

"Yes! No... I don't... I don't know, okay?"

"How do you know you're not strong enough anyway?"

"Because! I let those soldiers take mom... When dad left to fight, I promised him I wouldn't let anything happen to you or mom... that I would protect you..."

"Flicker... We were eight when dad left... I don't think he expected you to-"

"I've already lost mom and I don't wanna lose you too! Okay?" Flicker broke down and started crying but turned his back so his sister wouldn't see. "I... I can't lose you too... you're my best friend... I don't know what I'd do without you..." He suddenly felt an arm around his shoulders.

"I love you too," said Faun. "which is why I can't let you do this by yourself. Now let's go to sleep."

Flicker nodded, and the twins went back to their sleeping bags and fell asleep.

CHAPTER 7

CYNICAL

L A⊟⌐L ⅃L

FLICKER woke up at sunrise the next morning. His eyes were still puffy from crying the night before. He sat up and saw that Xi was already up. He watched her pull something from her backpack. It was round and had a purple glow to it, and Flicker decided that it was some sort of orb. He watched her silently.

She tapped twice on the side of the sphere and said the word, "ignitus," causing it to glow brighter. She then began to whisper into it. When she finished, she said the word, "extinguo," and swiped her hand across it. The glow immediately stopped, and she shoved it back into her bag.

"What are you doing?" Flicker asked as he stood.

She let out a short shriek and turned to face him. "Flicker! I... um... what are you doing awake so early?" she asked.

"I could ask you the same thing," he said, taking a step closer. "What's that?"

"What's what...?"

"That thing in your bag."

"Nothing."

"So why were you talking to nothing?"

"I have no idea what you're talking about. And I really don't appreciate you spying on me."

"Don't play dumb. I know you're hiding something."

"Playing dumb? You're the one who's playing dumb!"

"You're lying, and I can prove it. Give that to me!" he yelled, swiping at the bag.

"No!" she said, pulling away. "Leave me alone, you creep!" She began to walk away but turned back to look at him. "I can't believe this... I thought we were friends..."

"Yeah. I thought so too," he said, watching her walk away.

Once she was a good distance away from him, she crouched behind a boulder, and opened her bag. From it, she removed the orb. She said the word, "indespectus," and waved her hand over the orb. Immediately, the orb disappeared. It was still there, but only those who possessed magic could see or feel it. She put it back into her bag and went to wake up Faun.

"Hey, kid. It's time to get up," she said. "We've got a big day today."

Faun rolled over to face her and groaned groggily. "What's so special about today?" she asked with a yawn.

Xi chuckled. "Today is the day we infiltrate the prison."

The three packed up their camp and left. The flight there was silent. Once they had landed, they decided to come up with their plan.

Xi removed a blank map and her wand from her bag. She laid the map out, and waving her wand over it, said "Ostendo."

Suddenly, a blot of ink grew from the middle, and spread until it was a map of the prison.

"Here's the plan," Xi said. "Two of us will go in, and one of us stays here with Nero. We'll be disguised as guards."

"How will we get the guard uniforms?" asked Faun.

Xi held up her wand. "Invisibility spell, So I'll stay here with Nero while-"

"No!" Flicker interjected. "I'll stay here with him. You go with Faun... um... just in case you need magic..." Flicker still didn't trust Xi since he had caught her earlier that morning with the orb, whatever it was.

"Good idea, Flick!" said Faun.

"Yeah..." said Xi with passive aggression. "What a great idea..." She sighed. "Whatever. Flicker will stay here with Nero while Faun and I go inside. We find some uniforms and disguise ourselves as guards. The helmet should hide your antlers. We find your mom, and we get out of there."

"How are you getting out?" asked Flicker.

She stood and pointed to a tower in the corner of the prison courtyard. "That building is the east guard tower." she knelt back down and pointed it out on the map. When we're done, I'll wave to you from the top of that tower."

She reached into her bag again, this time pulling out a small shimmering purple stone. She tapped her wand against the stone and said, "indespectus." The stone glowed brightly, then dimmed back down to its original state.

"An Effusi Amethyst," she said, handing it to Flicker. "It absorbs magic and allows people without magic to use it. When I signal to you, get onto Nero, crush it in your hand and say these exact words; Effusi, exolvo, indespectus."

"Effusi, exolvo, indespectus. Got it."

Xi turned to Faun. "Ready?"

Faun nodded, and Xi took out her wand and took Faun's hand.

"Wait!" yelled Flicker, realizing he didn't trust her with his sister either. "I'm coming with you two! Nero should be fine here, right?"

"I guess so," sighed Xi in annoyance.

Faun went over to Nero and began to pet his beak. "Come for us when we get to the top of that tower, okay?"

The griffin purred in understanding and nuzzled her face.

Once again, the trio joined hands. "Ready now?" asked Xi. The twins nodded.

"Indespectus!" she said, and they vanished. "Languae magicae!"

Suddenly, everything went dark, and a loud ringing pierced through Faun's ears. She could no longer feel Xi's hand in hers. She tried to scream, but as she opened her mouth, she felt herself flatten, sending all of the air out of her lungs. It felt to her as though there was a layer of glass crushing her underneath.

One second, she felt that she would die, and the next, nothing. She tried to raise her hand in front of her face, but she couldn't feel it. It wasn't there. Nothing was. It was scary, but she preferred it to the deflated feeling.

All of a sudden, a bright flash of millions of colours passed in front of her eyes, and the glass shattered. She inhaled sharply and opened her eyes, feeling herself reflate. She bent over, panting heavily. She felt like she would puke. She noticed Flicker leaning against a pillar holding his head and breathing heavily.

"You okay, kid?" asked Xi, who also seemed very out of it.

"Mmhmm..." said Faun, nodding.

"Okay then," she said. "Let's keep moving."

CHAPTER 8

INFILTRATION

"REMEMBER you two, nobody else can see you," said Xi as they were about to leave the tower that they had ended up in.

They walked quietly past the courtyard full of guards standing around idly as the prisoners argued and fought. As they got inside, they walked under dripping pipes and past rats scurrying about in search of a spare crumb lying around. The air inside was musty and damp, smelling of sweat and mold.

Faun was disgusted and hated even the thought that her mother could be being held captive in such a place.

They finally made their way to the armoury and suited up over their clothes. Xi reversed the invisibility spell.

"Okay," said Xi. "Now I think we should split up. Just to cover more ground. Okay?"

Just as Faun was about to agree, Flicker interjected. "I'm not very sure I agree with that idea, Xi."

"Well that didn't sound passive aggressive at all!" Xi smiled. "Certainly not like you don't trust me, right?"

Flicker rolled his eyes. "I don't think it's a good idea to split up, Xi. I THINK we should just stay together, right Faun?"

"Well," Faun started, "I--"

"Well I THINK she agrees with me," said Xi. "Back me up here, kid."

Faun sighed. "Actually, I--"

"No! I'm her brother! She agrees with me!"

"No, she--"

"I CAN SPEAK FOR MYSELF, THANK YOU!" shouted Faun. "And at this point, I don't care what either of you do! I can't stand being around any of you right now!" She sighed. "I'm going by myself. DON'T follow me." With that, she stormed off.

Tension filled the air between Xi and Flicker. After a long, aggressive silence, Xi just turned, leaving Flicker with only the words, "I'm leaving."

"Whatever," Flicker mumbled, walking out.

Faun was walking alone down a corridor. She was a bit on edge about being by herself and regretting leaving alone. She was just going to turn back when she heard someone call to her.

"Hey newbie!" came the shout.

Faun turned to see a female troll walking in her direction. A bit panicked, Faun froze in place.

"What are you doing here by yourself?" she asked.

Faun remained silent, and just stared at her.

"Oooookay then... How about you come with me, kid? I'll show you around the place?"

She nodded.

They began to walk with each other out of the corridor.

"So, uh," said the soldier in an attempt to start a conversation. "What's your name?"

"F-- I-I mean... A-Azure..." She realised that she couldn't use her real name, because if she did, there was a chance she could've been caught.

"I like it. Mine's Jay."

As Jay continued to speak, Faun just looked over at a cell block, wondering if her mother could possibly be there.

"Hello? Are you even listening?"

Faun jumped a little but nodded.

"You don't talk a lot, do you?"

She shook her head.

"Shy, huh? Give it a week or so. You'll get used to working this place."

"Um... Jay?"

"Yeah, what is it?"

"Are there any Cerfinum here?"

"No clue. Why?"

"N-No reason. Let's just keep going."

"Okay. Let's go to the courtyard towers. I have to patrol there anyways."

"Um... Okay. Lead the way."

Meanwhile, Flicker had found his way to the canteen. He was just about to leave, as he didn't want to be distracted from his true goal, but just as he was headed for the door, someone yelled, "Hey new guy!" from across the room.

Flicker sighed. He didn't want to blow his cover and seem too busy, so he turned and walked over to them. He figured he could at least gather information from them.

"Come sit with us. You looked a bit lost back there. First day?"

"Uh... Y-Yeah!" he chuckled nervously.

"What's your name, new guy?"

"M-My name...? Oh! Uh, my name is... Kyro."

"Well, Kyro, you know you don't have to wear your helmet in here, right?"

He knew taking his helmet off would reveal his antlers and give away that he was not supposed to be there. "I-I know, but I... I have an embarrassing birthmark, so uh... yeah."

"Okay, now you gotta take it off," said one of the other guards at the table. "I have to see it."

"We promise we won't laugh," said the first guard.

"I might," giggled the second, who was already reaching over to knock the helmet off.

"No!" shouted Flicker. He raised his hand to knock hers away, but instead ended up knocking his own helmet off.

Everyone in the room turned, watching it fly into the air and fall, clattering to the ground.

The room went completely silent as all eyes fell on him. "He's a Cerfinum! Get him!" someone suddenly yelled.

"What type of powers do you think he has?" murmured another.

The guard who had first called him over walked up to him slowly. "Come with us peacefully, kid. We don't wanna hurt you."

Flicker pulled off a glove and grabbed the man's wrist, burning him. The man screamed, and Flicker tried to run away, but was blocked by a guard in every direction he tried.

The guards circled him. In a desperate attempt, Flicker held his hands as though he were holding something in them and tried to create fire. He knew this was his only hope at escaping them. All this was in vain, though, as every time he tried, the small flame he produced went out immediately.

He looked around before lowering his head in defeat. sprinted past them at the last second and headed for the courtyard.

"Go get the warden!" a guard shouted.

While all this had been going on, Xi had other plans than to look for the twins' mother. After she had left the changing room, Xi began walking towards the warden's office.

She walked in to see that the warden was with Prince Kaye, who was standing in the corner. "De'ekise-Sai and Royo Kaye," she said with a bow.

The warden spun his chair around to face her. "Xi," he said. "They're here?"

"Yes, sir."

The prince turned around to face her, revealing the burn on his neck and cheek from Flicker. "They will not be locked up here," he said. "I want to be the one to lock them away for assaulting me."

"Of course, Royo," said the Warden. "Xi, where are they now?"

"They're around the place looking for their mother. I told them she was here."

The warden smiled. "Good work, my daughter."

Xi smiled back at him. "Thank you, father"

Suddenly, two guards burst into the room.

"Warden! A-And, your majesty!" one said. "There's been an incident!"

"A young deer boy, a Cerfinum with the fire element, came into the canteen disguised as a guard and now he's running around the prison somewhere!"

"Xi," said the warden.

"Yes sir," she replied. She pulled the orb from her bag, which of course, nobody else could see, tapped her wand on it, and said the word, "revelare."

In an instant, the orb was now visible. "Ostende, Flicker." A foggy image of Flicker running through a hallway appeared inside of the orb. "I know where he is," she said.

CHAPTER 9

BETRAYAL

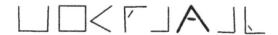

FAUN was walking with Jay, but when they got to the top, Jay told Faun to wait for her to finish her patrol in the tower.

Meanwhile, Flicker was just running, but he didn't know where to. Quite frankly, he didn't care. He just wanted to get away from the guards that were after him.

Somehow, he managed to find himself running up the same flight of stairs his sister had just climbed. He was going so fast that he ran straight into her.

"Flicker?!" she said, "What are you doing? Where's your uniform?"

"That doesn't matter right now," he replied. "You and Xi should finish the mission without me."

"Or I could just leave you both here," came Xi's voice from the stairway.

The twins turned to see her walking up the last few steps with her wand in her hand. She stopped at the top and leaned against the doorway.

Flicker stepped in front of his sister. "Dirty double crosser."

Xi chuckled. "Oh please. Like you didn't already know."

"I trusted you, Xi!" said Faun.

"Your mistake," she replied. "I truly didn't know I was such a good liar. Now, you two are coming with me. The prince you two assaulted is waiting in my father's office. He is very much looking forward to seeing you."

"Your father?" asked Faun.

"The warden," she replied.

"You told me your father had died fighting in the war!"

"And you still believed me after I betrayed you? Pathetic."

"So what about Brutus? And Xoe and Lucky?"

Xi scoffed. "I brainwashed them," she said proudly.

"Our Mother's not even here, is she?"

Xi just smirked. "Someone's finally catching on. Now come on. Don't make me use my magic."

Flicker tore off his gloves. "Don't make us use ours."

Xi laughed. "What're you gonna do? Hit me with imaginary fire? Or is your sister over there gonna crush me with her little pebbles? Come on, little deer boy. Burn me to a crisp."

Flicker's breaths grew deep. He bit his lip as he felt his hands begin to heat. "Shut up..."

"No. You and your weak sister couldn't do anything if you wanted to. And if you deny it, then blast me with your oh so powerful fire."

Faun fought her tears back and looked away.

Flicker took a deep breath and threw his hands forward at her. "Shut up!" he screamed, but nothing but sparks and a small flame flew from his fingertips.

"Poor thing can't even control his element. Go ahead! Do it! Hit me with your biggest fireball, Sparky!"

"I told you," he said, clenching his fists, "to SHUT UP!!!" Flicker shoved his hands out towards her, and an enormous ball of flame came flying out at her.

Xi instinctively dodged it, jumping out of the way. She stood up and glared at him. "Congratulations!" she said, "You've proved your point! Now let's go. You're coming with me one way or another, and I think we'd both prefer the easy way."

Flicker looked her dead in the eye, lit his hands up and said, "I think we both know that it's going to be the hard way."

Xi let out a deep overexaggerated sigh. "If you insist," she said. "Fove!" she shouted, pointing her wand at him.

Instantly, a ball of light flew from the wand, and Flicker jumped out of the way. He then tried to lunge himself at her, but she impulsively shouted, "Sobvolo!" and almost instantly, he began to float.

"I could use a little help, you know!" said Flicker whose back was now against the tower's ceiling.

Faun looked up at him. "I... I can't... Xi's right... I'm too weak..."

"No, you're not!" he said, throwing himself onto Xi. He knocked the wand from her hand, and it fell to the ground.

"You stupid brat!" she screamed, pushing him off her.

She tried to punch him, but he pushed her out of the way, angering her even more. She grabbed him by the shirt collar and flung him against a pillar in the corner.

Faun watched on in horror as her brother fell to the floor. "What did you do?!" she screamed.

"Shut up," snapped Xi as she walked towards Flicker. She stopped and stooped down in front of him to look him in the eye. "Didn't your mother ever teach you not to hit girls?"

Flicker looked up at her and chuckled. "I'm sorry. I didn't think that applied to the psychotic ones too."

"I'll give you something to laugh at," Xi said and kicked him hard in the stomach. "Pest..."

"Flicker!!!" yelled Faun, who ran to her brother's side. She looked up at Xi and clenched her teeth. "I hate you..."

"Join the club," she replied. "Now if we're done playing around, you two have people waiting on you."

"I'm not going anywhere with you," said Faun as she stood up. She glared directly into Xi's eyes; her insecurity replaced with rage.

Xi sighed in annoyance. "Don't tell me you're trying to play hero too."

Faun stomped her foot, lifting many small stones into the air.

"You think I'm scared of your pebbles?" asked Xi, folding her arms.

"You'd have to be pretty dumb not to be," Faun replied.

"You're one to talk," said Xi, when suddenly, a stone went flying towards Xi, hitting her in her head. "Ah!" she yelled.

"Darn those pesky pebbles," said Faun with a smile.

The stones then began to pelt Xi. She tried to dodge them but failed and began to see bruises all over herself. She grabbed her wand from the floor, inhaled deeply and bellowed, "Deflecto!"

An invisible force flew from the wand, sending all the stones, and Faun, flying backwards over the side of the tower.

BETRAYAL

"Faun!" Flicker yelled.

Xi just stood there in shock, staring at the ledge which Faun had gone over.

A deadly silence fell upon them. Both were at a loss for words.

Suddenly, the ground began to shake as though a miniature earthquake were in process. Then, it stopped, just as soon as it had started.

"What was that?" Xi asked.

As if in response to her question, a strong gust of wind blew in their direction. Both Xi and Flicker looked up to see Faun, rising atop a large stone slab which had saved her from her fall.

Xi pointed her wand at her, though her hand was trembling but before she could get any words out Faun stomped, sending a chunk of rock flying out towards her. It hit her hand, knocking the wand from it, and sending it soaring over the edge of the prison wall.

Xi watched on in horror as her wand fell beyond her reach, then looked back up at Faun. She noticed Flicker forcing himself to stand and watched as he created a small ball of fire, which he held in the palm of his hand.

Faun stepped back down onto the tower. She folded her arms and said, "If you still wanna fight, Xi, we're all for it."

Xi sighed and lowered her head. "No," she said. "I know when I'm beat." She had begun to walk away, but turned back in the stairway and said, "I hope you both know that this is not over." At that, she turned and left.

CHAPTER 10

BEGINNING

FAUN helped Flicker over to the Eastern guard tower. There, she signalled to Nero to come and get them.

"Where do we go now?" asked Flicker as he climbed into the saddle on Nero's back.

"Home, I guess," she replied. "We could try to salvage what's left of our house and rebuild the rest."

Flicker shrugged. "I guess we don't have any better ideas," he said.

Their flight back home was silent. Both, though they hadn't found their mother, felt a sense of accomplishment from the mission.

Faun had discovered that she had more power than she ever imagined she could. She had evolved both mentally and physically and learned not to be so naïve.

Flicker's powers had evolved as well, and the fact that they had not yet found their mother made him want to develop them even more, even if only to take revenge on the people who had taken his mother from him and robbed him off his childhood.

They returned to Equis, and with the help of the nearby villagers, rebuilt their home. Three years had passed, and the twins were now fifteen, and living on their own. Despite the passing of this much time, neither had given up the search for their mother. Faun spent almost all of her free time developing her powers. Flicker spent his time researching; trying to gather enough information to determine their Mother's location.

During the passage of these three years, Kree had gotten paralyzed during a battle. Prince Kaye decided that this meant that he was unfit to be king, and dethroned him, announcing himself the new king.

Faun had been making dinner one evening while Flicker was reading a book. It was an ordinary evening, but that suddenly changed when someone ran up to their door, frantically pounding on it.

The twins, startled, looked at each other in shock.

Flicker closed his book. "I'll get it," he said, getting up. He walked over to the door. "Hello?" he said.

"Please! You have to hide me! They're- They're after me!" came a panicked girl's voice.

Faun, filled with curiosity, stepped out of the kitchen to see what was going on.

Flicker opened the door and let her in. The girl was a unicorn- a pale girl with white hair, which had streaks of pinks and blues in it alongside her beautiful horn of the same colours- and she seemed to be about their age. She wore a filthy silk nightgown, which was now tattered and torn, and her bare feet were covered in mud. The frantic girl was attempting to stop crying enough to explain to them what exactly was happening.

"Hey, don't cry," said Flicker, trying to calm her down. "Who's chasing you?"

"The gremlins," she cried. "They took over the capital, but I got away, and now they're after me!"

"Why would they spend so much effort trying to catch one escaped person if they've already taken over the whole capital?"

Just then, they heard voices coming from the direction of the forest. "I saw her go through this way!" a very raspy voice said.

Faun stepped closer toward the girl, just to get a better look at her, and it was then that she noticed the thin golden stripe on her horn. "Because she isn't just any random person, Flicker," she said. "They're after her because this is Princess Railyn..."

Someone began to bang on the door loudly. "We know you're hiding her! Don't make us break down this door!" they yelled.

The twins knew then and there that they would have to decide. They looked at each other, then back at the door.

Flicker pulled off his gloves and shoved them down into his back pocket. His hands almost immediately engulfed themselves in flames. "You in?" he asked Faun.

She nodded and braced herself for the inevitable.

None of the three teens knew what would happen next. Flicker and Faun thought that their journey to the prison was the biggest quest they would venture out on, but little did they know, it was only the beginning.

The beginning of what?

It was the beginning of their journey to becoming the Saviours of Crietan.

Made in the USA
Coppell, TX
07 March 2021

51393494R00046